my secret camera

Life in the Lodz Ghetto

For Cathy, Miriam, Lewis and Sarah — F.D.S.

my secret camera
Life in the Lodz Ghetto

Photographs by Mendel Grossman

Text by Frank Dabba Smith

Introduction by Howard Jacobson

FRANCES LINCOLN

It is sometimes argued that in the face of sufferings as terrible as those recorded here, art has nothing to say. Mendel Grossman's photographs prove that the contrary is true: that a single image plucked from the chaos of history can move us to understanding no less than to compassion; that beauty is never absent from human beings even at the worst of times; and that such beauty is not wasted on us.

For these are beautiful photographs. That may seem to make no sense. How can images of inhumanity be beautiful? They have not only lost their liberty, these men, women and children of the Lodz Ghetto, into whose eyes Grossman's photographs make us look with exquisite pity and affection, as into the eyes of people we love. They have been systematically enslaved, humiliated, herded and branded like animals, compelled to wear that ancient symbol of Jewish shame, the yellow star, and ultimately, though they do not know it yet, will be prepared like animals for slaughter. Where is the beauty in that?

Well, there is beauty in the circumstances of the photographs for a start. Taken secretly, and at great personal risk, with a camera hidden inside Mendel Grossman's raincoat, they have for that very reason

a nervous, heroic, agitated quality, and they catch life in the Ghetto as though by surprise, free of self-consciousness or posing, without anything coming between the watcher and the watched. This makes the photographs unbearably touching. If the young boy in the peaked cap is unaware of any camera, to whom is he turning his anguished expression? To us? Isolated, it would seem, from all humanity, a woman in a yellow star scrubs the streets. We observe her, forever unobserved, as from the vantage point of angels. She is seen. She is remembered. Thanks to the photograph, the cruel futility of her occupation is given meaning for all time.

Yes, these studies break the heart. God help us if there is ever a time when they do not break the heart. But they strengthen the heart, too – and here is more of the beauty I speak about – because they show the victimized finding reason to laugh and joke, finding community and purpose even in circumstances you would think too horrible to bear. In the end that is what Mendel Grossman's secret photographs record most vividly – his subjects' inextinguishable appetite for life.

Howard Jacobson

I have a secret camera. I hide it under my raincoat. I have cut the pockets so that I can stick my hands through to use it. I open my coat just enough for the lens to peek out.

I have to take my photographs secretly because I am a captive in the Lodz Ghetto. Not even the bridges go anywhere else.

I must carry on taking pictures – how else can I tell you the real story of the thousands of men, women, boys and girls trapped with me in this terrible place?

I often stay up all night to develop films and to
make prints of my secret pictures. I have a darkroom
because my official job involves printing photographs
of Jewish workers for their identification cards.
I also take photographs of Jews in the Ghetto doing
their work. Some of these pictures are stuck into
special albums that we give to the Nazis. Our Jewish
leaders think that the Nazis will let us live if we remind
them again and again about how hard we work.

I have to wear the yellow star on my jacket
because I am Jewish. The Nazis have ordered
all Jews, whatever our age, to wear these stars.

The Nazis hate us because we are Jewish.
They surround us with barbed wire fences
and they watch us, too. We are trapped
inside a small space.

I secretly climb to the top of buildings to
take pictures of Nazi soldiers. My friends tell
me I shouldn't. They worry that the Nazis will
catch me. They also know my heart is weak
and I will become ill if I try to do too much.
My own pain does not matter. I must show
what the Nazis are doing to my people.
My pictures will tell the real story, even if I die.

Thousands of people pour into the Ghetto everyday. They come from all over Poland and other places in Europe that the Nazi army has conquered. They are confused and frightened. They have left behind everything that was familiar to them.

Nobody knows what will happen

from one moment to the next.

No one saw me take this picture. I took it from the inside of a building, looking down onto the street. I shook with anger to see children harnessed to carts like animals. Here, people are slaves.

I'm determined to make copies of this photo. I will give prints to my friends and I will hide the negative. One day the world will find out the truth of how these innocent boys suffered.

A woman scrubs the streets.

Such a tiny bowl.

Such a filthy street.

When will our slavery end?

In order to survive, my friend Sasha embroiders swastikas for Nazi army uniforms. Her heart sinks each time she sews this symbol of hatred. Everyone in her workshop is exhausted. Sometimes they are too tired even to talk to each other during their short break. They have learned that moaning about the soup doesn't make it taste any better, either.

Men queue up for bread.

The wagon driver throws the loaves to them.

Each loaf has to last for seven days.

Everyone is hungry.

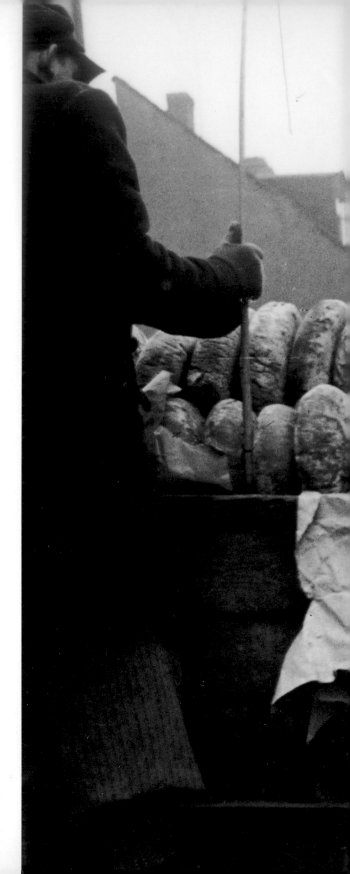

This young man has so little food,
and yet he shares it. In spite of our
suffering we help and care for
each other. And this girl still wears
a bow proudly in her hair.

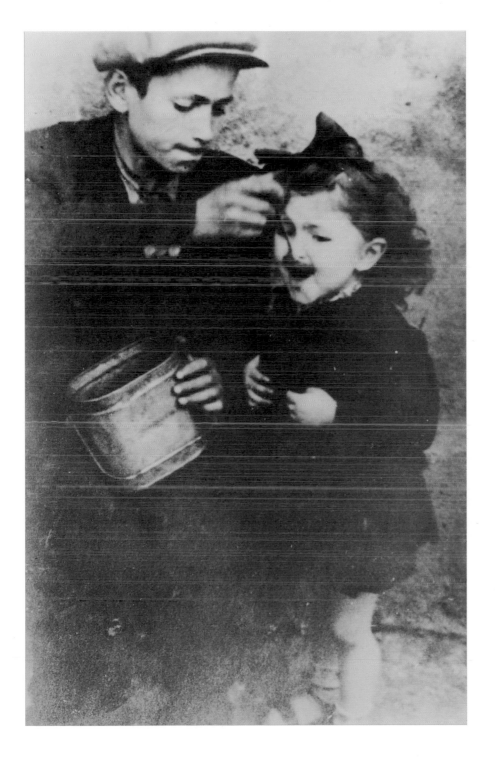

In April 1940, we baked matzos for Passover – the Jewish festival of freedom – in Lodz for the last time. On 1 May, a few days after we celebrated the festival, our own freedom was taken away by the Nazis. We are stuck in the Ghetto, surrounded by walls, fences and soldiers. But even though we are caged and hungry, we must be brave and remain free in our hearts.

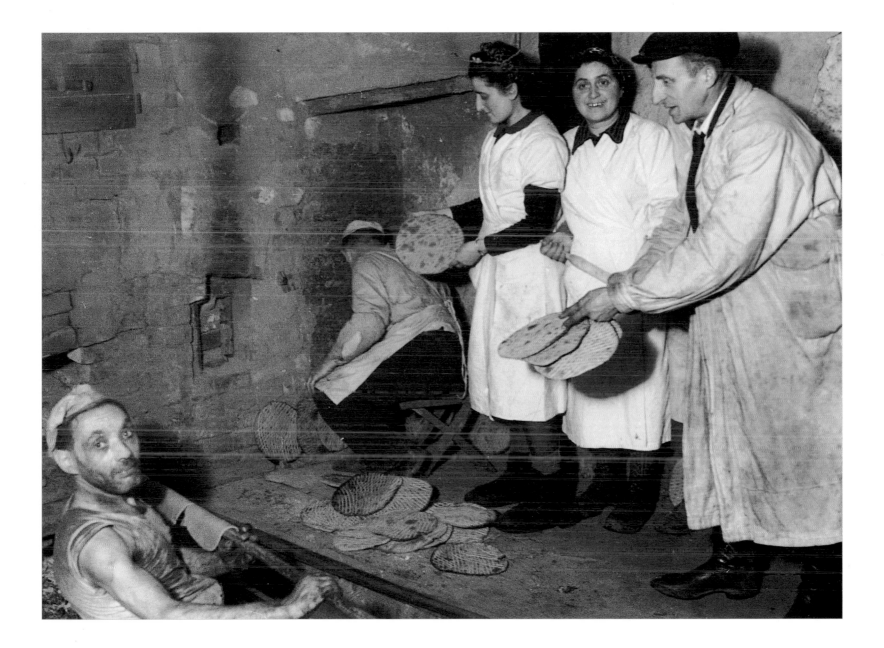

In spite of everything, we have to laugh
once in a while. We laugh at ourselves.
We make up funny songs, too.
Here, Jankele, a tailor from Poland,
sings with Karol, a travelling salesman
from Austria.

My friends Aharon, Arye, Aveya, Franka, Mark, Mirka and my sister Roska pose for a picture. They make me laugh so much that I don't hold my camera straight!

Just as thousands of people are forced to come in to the Ghetto, thousands are shipped out.

No one ever comes back.

Time and again I witness children left alone,
torn from their families.

A mother to her son: "Be strong, my boy."

Will we ever see each other again?

Mendel Grossman (1913-1945) was born into a Hasidic family and lived in Lodz, Poland. From a young age, he chose to devote himself to his photographs and drawings. After the Nazis conquered Lodz on 9 September 1939, he was driven by a passion to bear witness to the human suffering that was going on around him. Undaunted by poor physical health, the deaths of loved ones and threats from both Jewish and Nazi authorities, he produced a body of work that is unrivalled in its historical and compositional merits.

Shortly after occupying Lodz, the Nazis forced all Jewish residents to relocate to a cramped and filthy section of the city. The isolation of the Jews was complete when, on 1 May 1940, the Nazis sealed off the Lodz Ghetto from the rest of the city with barbed wire. Some 164,000 souls were trapped inside.

The Nazis set up a Jewish puppet government in the Ghetto to carry out their orders. The Ghetto became an urban slave camp. The Jewish leaders hoped that by marshalling a productive labour force, Ghetto residents would be spared further barbarities.

Grossman found employment in the photographic laboratory of the Ghetto Administration. Officially his role was to photograph, for example, products of the Ghetto workshops and identification pictures for work permits. This not only allowed him access to film and darkroom supplies, but also provided the perfect cover for his mission — to leave a day-to-day visual testimony of the genocidal tragedy enveloping him, and all those around him.

By the end of August 1944, those who had so far survived slavery, starvation and deportation were sent to their deaths at Auschwitz. During the final liquidation of the Ghetto, Grossman packed tin cans, containing around ten thousand of his negatives, into a wooden crate that he hid under a window-sill in his home. He had already distributed hundreds of prints in the hope that they, too, would survive.

Not long afterwards, Grossman died on a forced march from the prison camp to which he had been sent from Lodz. According to his friend, Arie Ben-Menachem, the artist witness still had his camera with him. After the Nazis were defeated in May 1945, Grossman's sister managed to locate her brother's hidden negatives and sent them to Kibbutz Nitzavim in Israel. Unfortunately, during the 1948 Israeli War of Independence, the Kibbutz was ravaged by the Egyptian army and the negatives were destroyed.

However, not all of Grossman's work was lost. After the liquidation of the Lodz Ghetto, the Nazis kept some prisoners behind as slaves. They were forced to eliminate evidence of the existence of the Ghetto. One of these men was Nachman Zonabend, a close friend of Grossman. He managed to safeguard Ghetto archives containing some of Grossman's photographs.

Today Grossman's compelling images may be viewed at the Museum of Holocaust and Resistance at the Ghetto Fighters' House in Kibbutz Lohamei Haghetaot, and at Yad Vashem, Jerusalem.

First published in Great Britain in 2000 by
Frances Lincoln Limited, 4 Torriano Mews
Torriano Avenue, London NW5 2RZ

British Library Cataloguing in Publication Data
available on request

ISBN 0-7112-1477-8

Set in Usherwood Book

Printed in Hong Kong

1 3 5 7 9 8 6 4 2

The author would like to thank:
Judith Levine, Photographic Archives, Yad Vashem, Jerusalem
Zvi Oren, Photographic Archives, Ghetto Fighters' House, Israel
Cathy Fischgrund, Susan Posner, Judith Escreet and Ellie Healey at Frances Lincoln
Anne Davies, Ivan Holmes and Nina Hess at Harcourt Brace